The Miracle of Love at Christmas

An Anthology of Short Stories and Poetry

Edited by: Claude R. Royston

ROYSTON
Publishing

BK Royston Publishing
P. O. Box 4321
Jeffersonville, IN 47131
502-802-5385
http://bkroystonpublishing.com

Published by: BK Royston Publishing LLC
Cover Design by: Customwebonline.com
Layout by: BK Royston Publishing LLC

ISBN-13: 978-0692292532
ISBN-10: 0692292535

Printed in the United States of America

Dedication

*This book is dedicated to
Any One Looking for the
Miracle of Love at Christmas...*

Acknowledgements

Special thanks to all of the authors who contributed to this book to make it a success.

Sylvia Carlton
Margaret Gilbert
Zachary Honey
Deidra F. Lee
Teresa Martin

A special thank you to my husband, Brian K. Royston for all of your love, care and support of the many books and projects that God places in our heart.

Rev. Claude R. Royston you are the best editor ever. Thank you always. To Mrs. Lillie Royston for your support, care and encouragement. To my awesome mother, Dr. Daisy Foree who is my number one cheerleader and will always have my back no matter what. You are the best mother ever. To my entire family for all that they do to keep me motivated and moving forward to fulfill this purpose in the earth.

We all need and want love. The best love comes from God above. Next, pour God's love on yourself and then spread God's love to everyone else. The greatest thing is still LOVE.

Love Always...

Table of Contents

Sylvia Carlton

THE GIRL NEXT DOOR

"The plane is about to make its descent into Chicago Midway Airport. Please fasten your seat belts and return all trays to an upright position. The flight attendants will be coming through to collect any items you wish to place in the trash. Thank you for flying with us. We know you have choices when it comes to your travel plans, and we are pleased that you chose Southwest Airlines." Ben stretched and looked out the window. He could see the snow-covered rooftops below. It was Christmas in Chicago and it was always cold, but beautiful. Ben smiled to himself as he thought of his Uncle Charles and Aunt Sarah. He was coming to visit them for the Christmas holiday, just as he had for the last three years. Ben was born and raised in Miami. He had never known cold and snow at Christmas time. He enjoyed having picnics on the beach on Christmas Eve and backyard cookouts during the holiday season in Miami. His family was small – just Ben and his mother in

Miami, and his uncle and aunt in Chicago. They had no children of their own, and had always spoiled Ben from the time he was born. He had a few other distant cousins, but he had long since lost track of them. But three years ago, just two weeks before Christmas, his mother had passed away from breast cancer. Since then, Ben could not bear to spend Christmas at home. So each year, he flew to Chicago to his Aunt and Uncle's where they would spend the holidays together. He loved the hustle and bustle of shopping at the malls, walking on Michigan Avenue watching, eating lunch at the Walnut Room Restaurant at Macy's on State Street and seeing children wide-eyed with wonder and anticipation as they gazed at all the decorations up and down the streets and in the store windows.

He arrived at the house welcomed by the smell of chocolate chip cookies baking in the oven. Aunt Sarah knew they were his favorite. He remembered her bringing him a fresh baked batch every time she came to Miami to visit. He had so many fond memories of his childhood, and he would never have believed in a million years that his mother would be gone so soon. He pushed those thoughts to the back of his mind as he sat his bag down in the foyer and hugged his aunt and uncle.

"Merry Christmas, Ben!" they said.

"Merry Christmas guys" Ben said as he looked around. "Wow, Aunt Sarah you have really gone all out with the decorations this year."

"Yes" she winked at Ben, "I decided to add a little something extra. We're having some special guests for Christmas dinner." Ben and his uncle exchanged a look, and Aunt Sarah knew exactly what they meant.

"I'm sorry," said his uncle as he shrugged his shoulders. "I told her not to try anything, but you know your Aunt Sarah. She's on a mission." Ben laughed and shook his head.

"Okay, Auntie, I'm going to freshen up. See you in a little bit."

Ever since her sister had died, Sarah had been concerned about Ben's social life. She of course understood the pain of losing a parent, but she told her husband that she was afraid that Ben would never get married or have children. Charles told her to just give him some time, after all it had only been three years, and that he would come around. But each Christmas, Sarah somehow arranged a dinner or an outing or an impromptu visit that always involved a young woman Ben's age. Ben and his uncle Charles always got a kick of it. They knew she meant well, and they also knew that they would not be able to change her. So they just played along. Secretly, Ben enjoyed the matchmaking "game" but so far, none of the women he met captured his attention enough to be more than a friend.

Ben was 20 years old in his junior year in college when his mom died. Now at 23, he was in graduate school pursuing his Master's in Education. His mother had been a math teacher, and Ben was following in her footsteps. He pulled out his phone and brought up her picture. He kissed it and said "Merry Christmas, Mom. I love you and miss you so much." Then he took a long hot shower and went downstairs to see if he could steal a cookie before dinner.

Dinner was wonderful, as usual. Sarah always had turkey, ham, green bean casserole, macaroni and cheese, corn bread, candied yams, assorted salads, cakes and chocolate chip cookies exclusively for Ben. "Get a good night's sleep," Sarah told Ben after they had finished dinner. "Tomorrow we hit Michigan Avenue to do some shopping." Ben always looked forward to that. He kissed his uncle and aunt goodnight and went up to his room.

The next morning they had an early breakfast and headed out. As they were pulling out of the garage, Ben caught sight of a young lady on the porch next door. He thought to himself he didn't remember seeing her on his visits before, and figured she must be visiting someone for the holidays. Their eyes met for just a few seconds, and she gave him a smile and turned away. Shopping on Michigan Avenue was great as usual, then on to lunch at Macy's and looking at the window displays on State Street. When they returned home, Ben glanced over at the house next door hoping that the girl would be there again. He laughed to himself thinking "How silly of you. She was probably someone visiting from who knows where and is most likely gone by now." But he couldn't erase from his mind that 3-second glance, the eyes, the smile. . .

Later that night after dinner, Ben tried to sound as casual as he could, "Aunt Sarah, is there a new family living next door?"

"Not to my knowledge" she replied. "Why do you ask?"

"Oh no reason. I just thought I saw someone on the porch that I didn't recognize. Must have just been someone visiting for the holiday."

"Probably so" Aunt Sarah said. "And speaking of visitors…"

"Oh no, here we go!" Ben laughed. He knew his aunt was about to tell him about her next match for him. "Let's hear it, Auntie. Tell me about this wonderful girl you want me to meet who you are sure I will fall madly in love with at first sight." He and Uncle Charles laughed. "That's okay," Aunt Sarah replied, "Laugh if you will, but this girl is very pretty. And she's studying to be a teacher, just like you. So right away you have something in common."

"Okay," Ben said. "So far, so good. Tell me more." He actually had started feeling that he might finally want to develop a relationship with someone. He was just starting to slowly get over his mother, and it would be nice to have a woman in his life. He was starting to feel that he was ready to share his life with someone. He thought again of the smile from the girl next door. Maybe he should try to find out for himself who she was. Aunt Sarah would be totally outdone if he did that!

"Well, this young lady is the niece of a couple at our church," Aunt Sarah continued. "Her name is Emily, and she is the same age as you. I invited them over for Christmas dinner, so you will get to meet her then. Just give it a chance, dear. I really worry about you, and I just want you to be happy."

"Okay, Auntie," Ben replied. "I'm looking forward to it." And he really meant it this time.

His uncle laughed again, "Well this is the third year in a row that your Aunt has tried to fix you up. Either it will be third time's a charm or three strikes, you're out!"

The next couple of days were filled with last-minute Christmas preparations. Aunt Sarah and Uncle Charles loved Christmas, and now that Ben was with them every year, they tried to make it extra special. Ben's room upstairs looked out over the front, and Ben found himself peeking out of the window a couple of times on the off chance that he might see his mystery girl. He wished that he could catch sight of her on the porch again, and if so, he was going to go over and introduce himself. No such luck. "Well," he chuckled to himself, "maybe this Emily person will sweep me off my feet, and the mystery woman will have missed her chance."

Christmas morning arrived, and it was wonderful as always. There was coffee and donuts, followed by exchanging gifts and then Uncle Charles playing the piano. He was actually quite good, and Ben never tired of listening to him. Finally Aunt Sarah went into the kitchen to put the finishing touches on her dinner. The guests were to arrive around 3:00 p.m. Ben went upstairs to relax for a while. It was around this time every year after opening the gifts that he really thought of his mom. His uncle and aunt understood, and always let him have his alone time. At 3:00 p.m. on the dot, Ben heard the doorbell ring. Although he still had his doubts, he had decided to have more of an open mind this year. He knew also that his mom would want him to be happy.

"Ben?" Aunt Sarah called from the bottom of the stairs. "Our guests are here."

"Ok, I'll be right down." He looked at his mother's picture once again and smiled. "Ok, Mom. Here goes nothing."

Ben walked into the living room where the couple from the church were sitting. "Ben," his Aunt Sarah made the introductions, "This is Mr. and Mrs. Preston from the church. This is my nephew, Ben."

"So nice to meet you, Ben," Mrs. Preston extended her hand. She was a very attractive woman. Ben thought to himself, 'If her niece looks anything like her, we might have something here.' "Likewise," replied Ben. He extended his hand to Mr. Preston, "Nice to meet you, sir."

"We would like for you meet our niece, Emily" Mrs. Preston said. She just went back out to the car to get a gift she brought for your aunt Sarah. Oh, here she is now." As Emily walked through the door, Ben froze in his tracks. He couldn't believe his eyes. Standing two feet away from him was the girl he had seen on the porch next door! She recognized Ben as well, and gave him that smile. Mrs. Preston noticed the exchange. "Have you two met before?" she asked.

"Not exactly" Ben laughed. "I actually saw Emily standing on the porch next door, and I asked my aunt if a different family was living there."

"Yes, I remember," Sarah joined the conversation. "I had no idea who Ben was referring to. I just assumed it had to be someone visiting the Smiths' for the holiday."

Mr. and Mrs. Preston both started to laugh. "Okay, we can explain" Mrs. Preston said. "As you know, Mrs. Smith makes quilts and I ordered one from her to give as a gift. When I came to pick it up, she was just finishing it. I still had errands to run, so I decided to come back for it in an hour or so. Emily was with me, and said she would just stay and visit with Mrs. Smith for a while until I got back. I called her when I was on my way back and she came out on the porch to wait for me. So that must have been when Ben saw her."

Ben could not believe his eyes, or his luck. Aunt Sarah was beaming. As they went into the dining room to have dinner, both Ben and Emily knew that this was the start of something good. Uncle Charles looked at Ben and smiled, "third time's a charm, I guess."

Margaret Gilbert

THE CONSPIRACY OF CHRISTMAS

Oh what has this world come to some

say? What have we done to Christ's birthday?

The day that was set aside to celebrate his

birth – has been lost to us here on earth.

Instead of honoring him – our love life has

grown dim.

We worship stuff and other things – we've

forgotten who is the real King!

We lost the spirit of the season – We get

excited for the wrong reason.

The flow is gone – no faith – no love – no

wellness in our whole life long.

What are we doing – he gave it all. Why can't

we keep just one of his calls?

How did we turn so far from the truth when

we've heard the word from our youth?

They preached it and – they talked it and even walked it out.

There's no way we did not get it – so how can we now not live it? It makes me want to shout.

What have we done with Christmas? How can we let it pass?

How can we give more to a pair of shoes than to a love that will last?

We clog the flow of his word – the blessed story that we already heard.

If we relax and let it flow our love for God's gift will soon again grow.

Through love and obedience and faith too.

Wellness and wholeness will again come to us like out of the blue.

In faith – in love – in obedience pure peace will be ours for sure.

Flow in the love that this day brings – you can do without the rest of those things.

Celebrate with all your might. Shout and sing

and run about. But give him the glory – it is his

birthday – it is his story.

Listen for his word. Obey without strife – to

insure kingdom living in this life!

Zachary Honey

The Star On The Tree

Though it ran fashionably late to the point of inexcusable tardiness, winter had nevertheless arrived. The trees with their pointy caps, the buildings with their shiny, sharp icicle necklaces, and the shrubs with their fluffy coats all adorned themselves in the white that was the fashion of the season. Each and every house was fully decorated in anticipation of the coming holidays. In one of these homes, a family had just finished constructing the centerpiece of their holiday and their Christmas tree was decorated from base to crown with an array of magnificent ornaments. At the very top of the tree sat a bright and shining star. The star was so bright, in fact, that the father of the house had to shield his eyes as he and his family admired the tree.

"I chose the brightest one I could find," the man's young son said beaming up at him. "Since it is at the top of the tree, where everyone looks first, I wanted the best and brightest star." The boy's mother smiled down at him and then to her loving husband. The father smiled back at his wife and all three were in agreement that on the very best of holidays, on top of the very best of trees, should sit the very best and very brightest of stars.

As the family spent the coming weeks preparing for Christmas, the Star continued to shine his absolute brightest. So bright was he that he very much distracted from the rest of the tree; but the Star was aware of this and he was actually quite proud. After all, he was the decoration that all spectators would notice first and remember always; and, being that he sat at the top of the tree, there was nothing above him that was of any great importance. So, in order to avoid disappointing any who looked at the tree, even without his notice, he always shone his absolute brightest.

Late one night while the family slept, the Star, illuminating the otherwise dark living room, looked about the house. As he surveyed the still room, he turned around to glimpse out of one of the house's many windows. To the Star's surprise he could see into a neighboring home that had a Christmas tree not unlike the tree on which he himself sat. Suddenly he was struck with a fit of jealousy. *'How could someone have a tree in the same line of sight as mine?'* He thought. *'Don't they know that my tree is the best of all?'* And then a most frightful thought occurred to him. *'Could their star be brighter than I? Surely not!'*

But the Star had to know for sure. He craned to see the top of the other tree. It remained just out of his view. He leaned further. Still unable to see the crown of the tree, the Star strained himself to lean just a bit further. But as he made this final arduous attempt, he fell.

Tumbling downward, the Star landed in the upper most branches of the thick Christmas tree. Out of breath, scared, and topsy-turvy the Star blinked open his eyes.

Staring at the Star with its arms crossed and its brow furrowed was a bright Red Bow. The Bow simply looked at the Star and said nothing. As the Star looked about he also noticed a White Bow hanging from a slightly higher branch. She also had her arms crossed and her brow furrowed. After a terribly long bout of silence, she spoke.

"Excuse me," she said with an air of arrogance that all bows possess, "but do you realize that while the world, in all its greater perfection, continues to go about altogether right-side-up, you remain completely upside-down?"

"Hrmph!" grumbled the Red Bow in agreement. "The way some people choose to live their lives these days is truly absurd. Did you know being right-side-up was the second thing I ever learned? I cannot remember the first, but I am sure it was not nearly as important."

"And I am most certainly not meant to be looked at upside-down!" exclaimed a beautiful and sparkling Snowflake who, though all her points were perfectly identical, always believed her top points to be the more spectacular. "Don't you know we snowflakes primp and preen to show off our most attractive features?"

"And all this time I thought it was to hide your unattractive ones." commented the Red Bow to which the Snowflake gave a disapproving huff and shimmied downward burying her lower points into the tree.

"I assure you," spoke the Star, "I did not purposefully position myself to be upside-down, but came about this unfortunate orientation quite by accident." He made a great attempt to turn upright, but made very little progress.

"Accident!" spat the Red Bow. "Anymore, everything happens by accident. No one does anything but wait for some great accident to occur. It is a truly idle world in which we live."

"I have to go quite out of my way to have any sort of accident befall me," said the Snowflake. "It is a most tiring affair to have anything accidental happen at all."

"Most certainly," replied the White Bow softly. "Accidents are a benefit of the lower branches, not a privilege of the upper."

"How wonderful it must be to simply bask in the rewards of our good labor," returned the Snowflake.

"Society has become as turned around as our good friend the Star," continued the White Bow in agreement, though as she spoke of him she did not so much as glance in the Star's direction.

"Excuse me!" the Star interrupted. "Don't you know I have fallen from the very top of the tree and this whole time you have only bickered with each other about unimportant things? I happen to like being a part of conversation and naturally the best place for a star is in the center of it."

"Oh you sorry, misinformed Star," replied the Red Bow. "Don't you know that we *are* at the very top of the tree? There is really nothing above us that is of any great importance." He then turned from the Star and continued to complain about the state of the world with the White Bow and the Snowflake.

The Star was taken aback by the rude and erroneous response. He had never been talked to in such a manner and he detested being ignored. Did they not know that he was the sole reason for the tree in the first place? Surely no one would come to look at know-it-all bows or preppy snowflakes. Again he made a great struggle to turn upright and this time he was successful. But as he turned, he again fell and tumbled much further down the tree. As he landed he was sure to land right-side-up so as not to create a great stir.

As he settled he noticed, to his delight, that he was in the middle of a great many decorations. All of them were abuzz with gossip and the chatter of conversation. He looked around and saw a jolly Red Christmas Ball reflecting everything around him. He noticed a military-style line of popcorn, all of whom had bulbous, bald heads and bushy white mustaches.

He saw many rows of lights who were all so shy that the moment he looked at them they would close their eyes and go out in a fright. He saw a beautiful Tinsel with her long locks of silk swaying back and forth to an inaudible melody. The Star continued to look around as he listened to their conversation.

"You see," said the Red Ball, "I am making a great attempt to know myself, and I am of the mind that in order for one to know oneself, they must first know about all others."

"On the contrary," rebutted a Popcorn, "How can one know anything of others if he does not know himself first? Surely in order to know about others, one must get to know oneself firstly."

"I certainly hope not!" exclaimed the Red Ball quite worried. "I fear that if I were to get to know myself first, I would find myself so interesting that I should have no reason to move on. You see, I am said to be something of an idol. A truly admirable trait if I do say so myself. Any who come to admire me sees something of them in me."

"It is true," spoke the relaxed Tinsel admiring her long locks in the Red Ball's reflective outer surface. "Although, to be perfectly honest, I do see myself in everything I look at."

"Well, at least you see something in the world," the Ball again continued. "It is good we are not all as fleeting as these lights who are so shy that they blink off half of the time. They miss half of everything that occurs." As he spoke of them, an eavesdropping Blue Light became so overcome with embarrassment that he shut his eyes tight and went out. And as lights are followers, the moment the Blue Light did this so too did the whole strand go out. "Tis a sad thing to miss out on the world," the Ball continued further. "I would be very sad to think of a world that I was only a part of half of the time. And I would be even sadder for all of my admirers."

"Ahum, Ahum!" interrupted the Star at last. "Excuse me, but you have all talked and talked this whole time, but I have come from the very top of the tree to tell a story of my own." When everyone had quieted and given him their full attention, he began.

"Once upon a time, when the world was very old and the night sky was but a bleak blanket of dark blue, a young Star showed up and noticed the depressing display which covered the earth. He traveled the world and witnessed all of the pleasant and wonderful people who inhabited it. But he could only be sad because though they lived in a marvelous and magical world, when people looked up at the night's sky there was nothing but nothing."

"When the Star came to the small village of Bethlehem, he was so overcome with grief that then and there he made a decision. He decided that it was his duty to give the people of the world something magnificent to look at. Something so that when they looked upward they would lose themselves in the beauty that hung above their heads. So he shone. And he shone brightly. In fact, he shone so brightly that it seemed all of the world could see him at once. And they were truly awestruck."

"The people of the world were so impressed with the Star's brilliance that some traveled great distances to bask under the Star's great light. Three men traveled for many days to bring the Star gifts in gratitude of his brilliant beauty. One family, pregnant with child, spent the night in a small, dirty manger directly under the Star's bright glow where the woman gave birth to a beautiful and blessed baby boy. *'Surely* a baby born under the magnificent light of the Star must be holy,' the world thought, and the child was considered the savior of all mankind.

"To pay homage to the magnificent Star, people celebrate once a year by putting a large tree in their homes. At the top of that tree sits a star, not unlike myself, representing the star that shone on that important night so long ago. During that time of the year, people throw magnificent parties and guests all come to view the wonderful spectacle that sits at the top of the Christmas tree."

Everyone was silent as the Star finished his story. In his usual manner, the Red Ball was the first to speak. "I am sorry," he started, "but I must point out a grievous error in your story, so unbearable that I completely stopped listening after you made it. For don't you know that we *are* at the very top of the tree? There is really nothing above us that is of any great importance." All at once everyone began to speak and argue with one another, and all ignored the Star.

Furious with the outrageous behavior of the other decorations, the Star silently and unnoticeably slid deeper into the thick tree. As he shuffled backward, he suddenly bumped into something and immediately heard a soft but forceful, "SHHHHH!" The Star turned around to see a small, withered Runner Sled.

"SHHHHH!" repeated the Sled. "Don't you dare give me away!"

"Give you away?" the Star returned in whisper. "What do you mean give you away? Are you hiding?"

"Yes of course I am hiding! And I should not like to be found. Not at the moment, anyway."

"Who may I ask is looking for you?" the Star asked as quietly as he could.

"The boy of the house of course! Who else?"

"But of course! Did you know it was the boy himself who chose me for the top of the tree? Most certainly for my brightness." The Star held up his chin with confidence.

"Blah! Stars. . . I never did care for stars. They are always competing to outshine each other. Every day there is only one star who shines the brightest and it is always the same one, the Sun. And she shines so bright that one must cover their eyes to look at her. Her brilliance renders her banal. Not to mention that she completely eclipses her friends causing them to become invisible. It isn't until night when all the stars become equally perceptible that their beauty truly shines. No, I would not shine like a star, but would prefer to stay hidden until the boy once again finds me and our game is ended."

"Would it not be easier to simply present yourself and end the game? If that is really the indeed the intended goal."

"Finding me is the end of the game, but it is, most certainly, not the goal." The Sled said.

"Are they not the same?" The Star asked.

"Foolish Star, have you never heard that *not every end is the goal. The end of a melody is not its goal, and yet if a melody has not reached its end, it has not reached its goal.* The same remains for this game of hiding and seeking which the boy and I play every year. You see, while the boy seeks me he must search every part of the tree. He must see every evenly knotted bow and he must glance over all of the beautiful blinking lights. He must watch, if only for a moment, all of the tinsel as it dances and sways. He must see his own reflection in the great round Christmas balls. In searching for something small and insignificant, he will inevitably see the whole tree. And that is the true goal. Sticking out and being found quickly would ruin the greater beauty that is the Christmas tree. I would dare not do such a wicked thing."

"Oh, you poor, misguided Sled," the Star replied with an air of overconfidence. "You must not realize that the only thing that interests the boy, and anyone else who comes upon this tree, is the thing that sits bright and brilliant at its peak, me."

"I am afraid it is you who are misguided, for the only thing that the boy cares about on this tree sits at the very bottom, well below its *bright and brilliant* peak. If you like, you may have a look for yourself, but please leave me alone for I fear you will have me found if we talk another moment." With that, the Sled turned away and said nothing more.

The Star was most offended. Surely the old Sled was mistaken. But to be sure, the Star decided he must look below and see the horrible goings-on for himself. As he leaned over and peered through the lowest branches into the very bottom level of the tree, the Star saw something most unexpected.

Below the all-important tree were stacks and stacks of presents, all different in size and shape. And just like the upper levels of the tree, they too were abuzz with conversation. However, it was conversation the likes of which the Star had never heard before. He was captivated as he sat observing it all.

"I assure you," said a Blue Present with yellow ribbon to a giant Purple Present with green ribbon, "your wrapping is most certainly the best I have ever seen!"

"Why thank you," replied the Purple Present. "You truly flatter me! But you, with your dress the color of the sky, are truly the form of Beauty."

"Oh now it is you who flatter me," replied the Blue Present and she blushed so intensely that she turned a vibrant red. "Now look what you have done."

"All for the better," said the Purple Present, and they laughed together.

Near the laughing gifts, a small and almost unnoticeable Little Box, tied at its top with a small piece of white ribbon, was sitting quietly alone; and, though he was not crying, he radiated sorrow.

"What is wrong?" asked a Giant Present, the largest in the whole stack. "No one should be sad this time of year."

"Oh," sighed the Little Box, "I was only thinking of how small and insignificant I am. I must be the smallest present to ever exist. How I envy your size, you must be the best and most valuable gift of all."

"Don't you know, Little Box, that size has very little to do with value. What is inside is what is truly important, and it is often the smallest gifts that are the most valuable. You, my little friend, may very well have a heart of gold or perhaps diamond." And he smiled down at the Little Box, and the Little Box smiled back.

Completely entranced by the conversations, the Star lost track of time. As he looked upon the world of the presents and listened to their humble conversations he was suddenly and quite unexpectedly plucked up out of the tree, raised all the way back to the very top, and placed once again upon the tree's peak.

At last, the Star was able to relax as an air of familiarity washed over him. With an exuberant exhalation, the Star gathered himself and prepared to shine brightly like only he knew how. But as he readied himself, he thought of his recent, grand adventure. He thought of the terrible bows and of the selfish snowflake. He thought of the loud red Christmas ball and the oblivious tinsel. He thought of how wickedly they had treated him and how they each believed themselves to sit at the very top of the tree. His face turned sour. But then he recalled the presents, all the way at the very bottom of the tree. He thought of their abnormal conversations and of how peculiar it was that they never once even thought about the tree or the all-important decorations that existed just above them.

And while he was quite sure that he was in fact at the top of the tree, his eyes couldn't help but drift upward to see if above him there might just be anything of some importance. As he looked up, his eyes peeked out a window into the blanket of dark sky. In an instant he was agog as he looked up at the hundreds upon hundreds of lightly twinkling stars that littered the night sky. How a vast number of insignificant specks could work together to make something so beautiful was beyond the Star's comprehension.

As the Star looked perplexedly into the beautiful array of twinkling sky, the whispers of the Sled came back to him. And as he thought of the poor old Sled, somewhere in the depths of the tree hiding with all his might, the Star came to understand the Sled's wise words. With a spark of inspiration, the Star, much like the star of his own story, made a decision. But unlike his idol, the Star did not choose to shine brightly, but rather he chose to dim.

"I'm sorry," the father said to his son having just placed the star back in its rightful spot on the tree. "The star must have broken when it fell. It doesn't seem to be as bright as before. I'll take it down and we can get another one tomorrow."

"No!" the young boy said grabbing his father's arm. "I think I like it better this way."

The father smiled down at his son and looked back at the tree, "You know, I think I do too."

With a dim star, each decoration on the tree stood out just as much as every other. The father and son looked at the tree and saw the gentle swaying of the tinsel and the beautiful knots of the red and white bows. They marveled at the glittering snowflakes and the way the Christmas balls reflected the slow flicker of the lights. They admired the strand of popcorn as it spiraled up the tree from its wide bottom to its pointy top. And because of the selfless act of the Star, it truly was the best and most brilliant tree that ever was.

After all, it is well to remember, from time to time, that were it not for bows and tinsel and blinking lights and strings of popcorn and large red balls and hidden runner sleds, a star would be a very silly thing to have sit atop a tree.

Deidre F. Lee

List of Characters

Parents

Lydia Lopez – Matriarch of the family. Married to Rico Lopez until his death. Mother of Matt, Nakita, Nadira and Malachi. Grandmother of Isabella, Imira, Illycia, Malik, Manuel, Monche, Michelle and Monique. The host of this Christmas Dream.

Rico Lopez– Husband of Lydia, now deceased. He is the father of the Matthew, Nadira, Nakita and Malachi.

Children

Matt Lopez – The oldest son. Married to Allyce, father of Isabella, Imira and Illycia.

Nakita Lopez – The oldest daughter. She has been in a relationship with Travis Johnson for several years. They are the parents of TJ and Tierra.

Nadira "Dira" Lopez – The youngest daughter. Currently single, formerly in relationships with Kendrick and Armani.

Malachi "Chi" Lopez –The youngest son. Currently single and the father of Malik, Monche', Manuel, Michelle and Monique (Lil Nique).

The Others
Consuela – Matt and Allyce's nanny. She has been raising Isabella, Imira and Illycia as their parents work on their careers.

Allyce Lopez –The wife of Matt Lopez and mother of Isabella, Imira and Illycia.

Travis Johnson – The boyfriend of Nakita Lopez and the father of TJ and Tierra.

Collette – Malik's mother and a former girlfriend of Malachi.

Tre' – Collette's husband and Malik's stepfather

Celeste – Manuel's mother and a former girlfriend of Malachi

Nicolette "Nickie" – Michelle's mother and a former girlfriend of Malachi

Monique - Lil Nique's mother and a former girlfriend of Malachi

Melanie – Monche's mother and a former girlfriend of Malachi

The Christmas Dream

"These bows, ughh! They are getting annoying." I mumbled as I tussled with the shiny silver wired ribbon. "There, perfect. Gifts wrapped. Let's see: house cleaned-check; Christmas tree up – check; lights on the tree – check; grocery shopping done-check; ornaments and wreaths in the living room-check; dessert and candy bar ordered- check; rooms ready- double check. Let the holiday begin," I chuckled. I swear after each item I checked off on my to-do list, my smile grew wider and wider.

It's been five years since I got to spend Christmas with all of my children. Between school, careers and raising their own children, my bunch-four in total were never home at the same time anymore. This year was different. On a family video chat back in the summer, the kids decided that everyone would meet here and spend the holidays together. Seven days together under one roof- kids, grandkids and me. Who knows what will happen but I am looking forward to every minute of it.

Since becoming an empty nester I've adopted a dog – a pure bred Rottweiler named Sampson. He helps me workout everyday – I'm up to a seven mile run with him every morning. He's even excited about the visit. He keeps roaming from room to room sniffing and looking for the grands – they love to play with him and he loves the attention. "This is going to be great!"

Ding, ding, ding the doorbell rang. "Ma! Ma, are you here?"

"Matt is that you?? Baby you're home it's so good to see you." I hugged him for what seemed like forever.

"Ma, how you doin' darling? So good to see you." Matt said. Allyce, Matt's wife was coming in shortly behind Matt.

"Allyce, girl, have you lost weight? I'm so glad you could come. We have to whoop these boys in Bid Whist like we did at the family reunion."

"Yes, we do. Tomorrow though, that flight with the girls wore me out." Allyce said.

"Hun, I understand. Rico and I took a car trip one time with all the kids – only one time," I laughed. I hadn't thought about that trip to Portland, Oregon in years. Four children, two adults and way too much luggage in a 4 x 4 SUV – oh God! That was the longest two weeks of our lives.

"Where's Consuela? I just knew you would bring her, too?" I asked.

"Mama, we gave her the holiday off to spend time with her family – she's earned it." Consuela, Matt and Allyce's nanny, usually traveled with them on every visit. "I think it's wonderful she gets some time off."

The girls – Isabella, Imira and Illycia had slipped past us heading to the game room in the basement and Sampson had followed. We could hear them laughing and him barking, so we knew everything was fine. Matthew nicknamed Matt is my oldest son. He and Allyce met in college and married the day after their master's degree graduations – his in journalism, hers in public relations. He is a correspondent for ESPN and Allyce is a public relations consultant. They currently live in Boston, Massachusetts near Newberry Street, the primo shopping area. Allyce hates the winters there. Originally from Atlanta, Georgia she has never gotten used to the level of ice and snow there since their move four years ago. We hung out in the living room, watching television. Within an hour, I was putting blankets over Matt and Allyce, they were exhausted.

"Girls, want to help me make dinner?" I asked them.

"Yes, Nanna here we come!" It was Isabella, the oldest yelling from the game room. At 10 years old she was almost as tall as her mother. Thin with a mocha brown skin, long dark brown hair and eyes Isabella had the look of a child actress. As the oldest she was in charge of her sisters when Consuela wasn't around.

"Imira and Illycia, do what Nanna asks you to but don't touch any knives, Consuela has told you before you're too little for that." Isabella said warning them both like she was suddenly in charge.

"You're not our boss, Isabella ", said Imira.

"Yeah, you can't tell us, what to do", Illycia screeched.

"What did Consuela say before she went to her family's house?" Allyce asked.

"Girls, listen to Bella. She's the oldest; she knows best until we are all home again." I stood there in awe. Isabella has grown from a funny, wobbly infant into a miniature adult. I wasn't sure if I liked it.

We made homemade deep dish pizza, a green salad and chocolate chip cookies for dessert. When everything was ready, I sent Imira to wake their parents and just as they came to the kitchen we heard.

Ding, ding, ding rang again. "Mama where is everybody?" Suddenly more family arrived.

"Which one of my crazy siblings is here?" Matt yelled.

"Dira, we're in the kitchen. Mama and the girls made pizza. Come on back." I said.

"Oh, no 'big hungry!'" an affectionate name we called Dira, "has beat me to dinner, I won't get anything" she laughed as she hugged Matt around his neck.

When she let go, he stood up and hugged her. "You need to answer your phone some time big brother."

"I know, I know I'll do better." Matt admitted sheepishly.

"Allyce," Nadira said to Allyce with that sarcastic tone she got when she really didn't like you. "Nadira, girls give your Auntie some love."

Dira ignored Allyce's tone and focused on the girls. "My princesses how are you? It's been too long let me take a good look at you. Bella, my goodness you've got so tall how old are you now, ten or eleven?"

"Ten Antie! I will be 11 in February." Bella answered proudly.

"Imira are you still playing soccer?" Dira inquired.

"No Antie now I dance – ballet mostly." Imira did a slight twirl right there in the kitchen.

"Well give me some notice and I will come to Boston for your show." Dira meant it. She would do anything for the girls.

"Yeah Antie, really?" The excitement was on Imira's face as she looked at Antie and her mom.

"Of course Sweetie, if it's ok'ed with your mommy?" Dira looked at Allyce with hope in her eyes.

"You're welcome Dira any time, you know that." Allyce said agreeably. "Ok, ok the pizza is getting cold." Allyce announced.

"Let's eat then," Nadira exclaimed. She and Matt sat next to each other, laughing and joking and telling the girls old stories from their childhood.

Nadira, my baby girl, recently graduated from an entrepreneurial MBA program at Tennessee State University. She has a million ideas but can't decide which one to start first. She also just ended a three year relationship, the longest one so far. Surprisingly she didn't seem too upset about it. Nadira announced about a week ago that she would be moving to New York City in the spring. She thinks it is the place for entrepreneurs. I'm glad she will be close to Matt. He has taken care of her, since Rico died when she was 12. They are the closest of all my children and I know he will look out for his baby sister. Nadira lives here in town but she said she would drop by for dinner and evening festivities during the holiday visit. She even said she would spend the night Christmas and New Year's Eve!

"Mama, when will Malachi and his tribe get here? Are any of his baby mamas coming?" Dira asked with that devilish eye.

"Dira stop it. Malachi and the kids will be here in the morning and NONE of the baby mamas, girlfriends, or wifey of the week will be here," I laughed.

"Ma how many does he have now? Five, two girls and three boys now."

"Uh huh, that boy has done too much." I said. "I know but they are your two nieces and three nephews just the same."

Turning to my two eating grands I asked, "Girls are you finished eating?"

Isabella looked at her sisters and said "We're done Nanna."

"Good. Take your sisters, some cookies and Sampson downstairs, grown folks need to talk." Suddenly I needed to dismiss the small ears in the room.

"Yes, Nanna. Come on sissies, come on Sampson." She grabbed half the cookies and led everyone downstairs. Soon there was laughing and barking coming from downstairs again.

Nadira was very upset with Malachi. As the baby, he was given every opportunity both from me and his older siblings. When he was in high school, Chi was an All-American first baseman and a great batter with a .350 average. He received a full-ride scholarship to Arizona State University where he majored in two things −women and baseball. By the end of his sophomore year Malik and Michelle were born. Manuel and Monique were conceived shortly before he was put on academic probation. With the help of several tutors he rallied back, just in time for Monche' Lydia to come into the world. At 23 years old, my youngest has five children and five baby mamas to contend with. Baseball scouts loved his abilities but were concerned about his personal life and his image. He wasn't quite ready for the majors so the Minnesota Twins sent him to the Toledo Mud Ducks for training and development. He's been called up for the next season. Nadira is upset with him and his choices. On a separate video chat, I convinced all them to allow Chi to bring the children here without any female. I just hope he stick to that agreement. This will be the first time he will have all of them together alone. This will be interesting.

"Mama what about Nakita? When is she due in? Is she bringing him again?" Matt never liked his other sister's man. Nakita is my oldest girl. When she left for college, she said she was getting a degree in social work. Seven years and two children later, she is still 45 credit hours short of graduation. She met Travis Johnson at the end of her sophomore year, he was a junior. The standout running back at Wilberforce University opted to forego his senior year and enter the NFL draft. It was a smart move for him – he was picked in the first round 15th by the Philadelphia Eagles. By the time he went to his first training camp, Nikita was pregnant with Travis Jr aka TJ. Travis asked Nikita to *move* to Philadelphia with him. Against my advice, she did. Eighteen months later, Tierra Nadira was born.

They agreed that Nikita would be a stay at home mom until the children started Kindergarten, essentially putting her dreams on hold for his. TJ is going to the second grade and Tierra will start Kindergarten in the fall. I'm anxious to hear when Kita will be going back to finish her degree.

"She will be here Thursday. Be nice Matt; don't cause tension like the last time." I reminded.

"Tension? Me, Mama? Not me, if he would be a man and put a ring on my sister's finger and show her the respect she is more than due, I would have no beef with him at all. Did I tell you he sent me tickets to the game against New England? I sold them." Matt said proudly.

"See that's what I'm talkin' about. Do I agree with your sister's choices? Of course not, but they are hers. She didn't have to move to Philadelphia. She didn't have to get pregnant again. She didn't have to put off her dreams – those were all her choices. Stop blaming Travis – she made her bed." I said.

"Let's agree to disagree mama, I won't mess up this holiday for the family but the first of the year –

that's another story." Matt said not wanting to argue with his mama on this wonderful holiday.

"Ok, Matt. You are going to do what you want to but she's grown now. She doesn't need you to fight her battles for her anymore." I said.

We decided to hang the wreaths that night. There are six doors to the house so we picked our favorites and drew straws for which one went on which doors. About an hour or so later, we were back in the living room listening to music and drinking Chardonnay. It was late when Dira decided to go back to her place. She kissed me and Matt, waved at Allyce and said "I'll be back around lunch time, Mama you need me to pick up anything?"

"No baby, thank you. See you tomorrow. Love you."

"Love you too, call you in the morning." Dira left quickly out the front door.

"Well Matt, I'm tired. I'm off to bed. See ya in the morning." I may have moved slowly to my bedroom but, by the time my head hit the pillow, it was over.

The next day I woke to Sampson licking my hand. It was time for our run. When I came back, the girls were at the kitchen island with pancakes and sausage in front of them. "Morning princesses." I said very lovingly to angelic faces.

"Morning Nanna," they said in unison as if they rehearsed it.

"Something smells good. Who fixed breakfast?" I asked.

"I did Nanna" Isabella beamed with pride. "Would you like some I have more batter?"

"Thank you sweetheart but I'll fix it."

"Its fine Nanna, I like to cook."

"Well ok then." Isabella carefully removed a large silver mixing bowl from the refrigerator and placed it on the counter. She went in the freezer.

Suddenly she turned around and said, "How many sausage patties would you like Nanna and do you want turkey or regular kind?"

"Three and turkey, please." I sat on the stool closest to the counter in case she needed me, and watched Isabella create one of the best breakfasts I've ever had. "Who taught you this sweetheart?"

"Consuela, Nanna. I asked her to teach me to cook about a year ago. I can make this, cornbread, spaghetti and meatballs and baked chicken."

"It's really good sweetie."

"Thank you Nanna." I cleared the dishes, loaded the dishwasher and cleaned the counter. Wow, she *is* a miniature adult.

It was about 11:30 in the morning when I heard "Mamasita, Chi and crew are here let's get the party started!!!" There he stood. My baby boy was all grown. At 6'2" and 200 pounds he looked like a statue.

"I shouldn't have to wear stilettos to kiss my son", I said laughing. He looks just like Rico when we were young. His Puerto Rican side was evident – curly black hair, golden brown skin and his Spanish accent. All the children were bi-lingual since birth but you would think Chi had lived on the island all his life.

"Look at my shugas. Hi kids how did you like the flight?" I asked.

"Nanna I took three planes to get here – two to daddy's and one here." Malik lived in Reno, Nevada with his mother and stepfather.

"Wow that was a lot 'Lik, I'm so glad you made it."

"Nanna are my cousins here yet? I've missed Bell since last summer."

"Yes Monche', baby they're downstairs with Sampson I think." With that I got attacked with hugs and off the crew went.

"Mommy, how's my favorite woman?" Chi asked as he hugged again.

"I better be the only woman this week Chi." I said.

"Mommy of course I will be a good boy – for a week," he laughed. I on the other hand wasn't amused.

"Chi I mean it. I promised ALL of those women there would be no one paraded in front of their children, you will respect that." I repeated.

"Mommy did you forget that they are MY children too?"

"So, that doesn't entitle you to do whatever in front of them. You know what? We are not having this conversation. You know better than the mess you do and you choose to do it anyway. Rico would be so upset to see this mess. But we are going to have a pleasant holiday for my grandbabies sake if for no other reason, right?"

"Yes, mommy, I promise no stupidness this week." He kissed me on the forehead and started his first trip with luggage to the bedroom. It took three trips before he was finally done.

"Damn, we had eight suitcases. No wonder the skycap looked so funny about that $10 tip. He deserved $50. How've you been mommy, really? I worry about you alone in this house." Chi stopped briefly to inquire.

"Chi, sweetheart, I'm fine. I have Sampson to protect me not to mention that gun Rico made me learn to shoot. Plus I'm not always in the house. I have Zumba class and plenty of friends to go out with. I'm still involved in the women's ministry at church and I'm thinking about going on a mission trip to South America next spring. I'm still very busy – just not taking care of the four of you now." He smiled. He always worried about me, ever since he was little. I remember on his first day of Kindergarten and he looked at Rico and said 'Poppy I can't leave mommy here by herself, she'll be sad,' Rico and I assured him it would be ok, that would be fine but as soon as we got out of the school building we laughed all the way home. The thought of that concerned face still makes me smile.

"Now tell me about you Chi. Have you found a place in Minnesota yet? When does training start? How are you getting along with kids' mothers? Are there anymore on the way?" I asked at a side glance.

"Mommy really no, I'm done having kids. This bunch is *enough*. Five kids in three states none anywhere near me – nope I'm finished. I had enough frequent flyer miles to get two of them here. It's ridiculous. I found a great house in Minneapolis. It has four bedrooms, four baths, an in –ground pool. It even has a house for you and Sampson mommy. I would love to have you there with me. Training starts in Florida in February. As for these crazy women I had children with - hmm it's interesting. Collette, Malik's mama is doing great. She's gotten her law degree and should be taking the bar exam the first of the year. She and Tre' love Reno, especially the weather. We get along and we try to do what's best him. Manuel's mother, Celeste is just crazy. Anytime she hears that I'm going to visit one of the other kid's she wants to put me back in court for a support raise. The judge is so sick of it that he said if she comes with one more frivolous request, he will cut Manuel's order. Manuel goes to private school, on the AAU traveling soccer team, plays the saxophone and plays chess. I pay for all of it on top of the support and it's still not enough. Nicolette is doing well, too. She has two other kids now, boys. Nickie lets me see Michelle regularly. She even let her spend last summer with me in Toledo. I should have stayed with Nickie. She was the only one who really cared about me. Monique is Monique, that's the best I can say. Lil Nique is six and she's still mad about Monche'. I've apologized a million times but anytime a conversation isn't going her way, she cusses me out about it. I was surprised she even let her come. Monique made it perfectly clear that lil' Nique would never be around Monche' and lil' Nique told me so on the plane. The baby said 'I can't sit by my baby sister because my mama will get mad. What kind of mess is that? Melanie, on the other hand wants Monche' to know all her brothers and sisters. She doesn't like Monique either but she doesn't want that to affect the girls' relationship. She's a real grown woman." Chi informed.

"Baby brother! I thought I heard you on the stairs," Matt yelled.

"Matt what's up? It's been a long time bruh. Where's Allyce? Don't tell me you finally left her."

"There you go – no. She's in the bedroom on a conference call. Where are your kids? Did all of them make it?"

"Yeah, they're downstairs with your girls and Sampson." All of sudden, we heard a roar of laughter coming from the basement. The boys laughed, too.

"They are having a ball." they said in unison.

Then I laughed. "You boys got dinner right?"

"Mommy for real? Mama what do you want for dinner? Come on Chi we can get it together. Ok mommy what do you want?" Matt asked.

"Fried Catfish, Cornbread, Steamed Corn On the Cob and Green Beans." I rattled off the menu easily.

"Whoa mama for real?" Matt looked concerned.

"Yes baby that was always the best meal you two made."

They looked at each other and I could sense their fear, "Ok mama anything for you. Guess we better start in an hour. Cool, mommy is everything in the same place?"

"Yes Chi, I haven't moved a thing."

An hour later, the clanging and banging began. Allyce came flying down the stairs "What is all the noise about? Is mama ok?"

"Yes Allyce. She's fine. Chi and I are cooking dinner."

"You cooking? I haven't seen you do that in at least two years."

"Don't ask me I forgot how. Mama asked us to do it. I have to say me and lil bruh have been having a ball."

"Malik, come here son!!"

A few seconds later, "Hi Antie. Yes Dad?"

"Y'all get that downstairs cleaned up. I know it's a wreck and then get washed up for dinner. Help Monche' she doesn't know how."

"Yes, sir." Going down the stairs we heard, 'We got to get everything cleaned up. Our daddies are fixing dinner.' We heard thumps and bumps and mumbling – a lot of mumbling.

About thirty minutes later, they emerged from the basement, ready to eat. As if on cue, in walked Nadira sniffing. "Catfish? Cornbread? The boys must be cooking."

"You know it!" Matt replied. "*Somebody* had to learn to cook mommy's favorite meal? Hi sis, get a plate," Chi said as he smirked at his sister.

"Nah, bump that. Mommy, the lady of the house should have the first plate. Want me to fix yours for you?" Chi offered.

"Some things never change – Chi is still in love with mama." I said proudly.

"I sure am and I'm gonna stay that way." Chi said.

"Y'all stop. Chi, baby I can fix my own thank you but I want all the children served first this time. Kids line up and let's get these plates together."

"Yes ma'am!" they all yelled.

Just as we had served up the last plate I heard, "I hope y'all saved some for us." More family entered the kitchen.

"Kita, TJ, and Tierra!!!" I exclaimed.

"Of course we did there's plenty on the stove. Where's Travis?" I asked.

"He'll be here in about 3 hours, some last minute contract negotiation. He didn't want all of us to be late. Kids say hello to everyone." Nakita said.

"I don't know them mama. You said not to talk to strangers." Tierra said matter-of-factly.

"Tierra this is your family – on mommy's side. Don't you remember your Nanna?" Nakita prodded.

"Yes, she's over there." She pointed to me. "I don't know the rest of them mommy." Tierra insisted.

"Well let me introduce you – This is your Uncle Matt and your Uncle Chi and your Antie Dira and you Antie Allyce. They are my brothers and sisters." Nakita said settling the situation.

"Hi." Tierra said dryly.

"Hi Tierra, it's been a long time. I haven't seen you since you were a baby." Dira said with a smile.

"Hi Tierra, I'm your Uncle Matt. This is my wife, your Antie Allyce. You're right you haven't met us before but I think you spent some time with our girls – Isabella, Imira and Illycia? I'm looking forward to getting to know you."

"I remember them. They stayed at our house for my birthday. Oh I see them now. Mommy can I go talk to them?" Tierra said after she saw the cousins she knew.

"Wait pretty girl, what about me? I'm not a stranger." Chi said.

"Uncle Chi!!!! Where's Che?"

"Hey pretty girl she's in the basement with the other kids. I have another little girl and 3 sons. You have lots of cousins here to play with." Chi informed.

"Mama when is daddy coming?" interrupted TJ.

"Is he *really* coming?" Chi asked.

"TJ can you say hello to your family?" Nakita redirected.

"Hello. Mama?" TJ said with a quick wave to all in the room.

"Yes he's really coming. Go wash your hands and eat." We fixed the kids their plates and off they went with the others. Nakita got a plate and it was just like the 'old days – laughing, joking, and telling on each other for things long forgotten. I hadn't laughed that much in months. Then Matt decided to play detective.

"Sooo, Kita how old is Tierra now? Five or six right?"

"She's five Matt. Her birthday was last month – not too late to get her something.   Chi even remembered and gave her a doll."

"Chi can you remember your crew's birthdays?" Nadira said in that nasty tone she gets with him.

"Their birthdays are December 22nd; March 6th; June 24th; August 22nd; and October 10th – anything else? I have everyone's birthdays in a book at the house and on my tablet. Kita made sure that she and her kids came to at least three of my games to cheer me on. One playoff game was close to her birthday so I made sure I had a gift for her at the ball park like I do for Nique and Manuel." Chi proudly notified all who cared.

"Don't you two start again. It's not a good look for adults. Matt why were you asking about Tierra's age?" I asked.

"Didn't you tell me that you were back to school when she turned five?" Matt asked.

"No what I said was when Tierra started Kindergarten I would finish and I am – as soon as Travis figures out where we're going to be living. He may be getting released from the Patriots." Nakita said.

"Tell him to try out for the Vikings, it would be nice to have you and the kids close again." Chi said.

"Close again, Chi what are you talking about?" I said. "

Well at the beginning of the season, Kita stays with me some times with the kids 'til Travis gets back from training camp." Chi said.

"Travis doesn't like for me to bring the kids to training camp. He says we are too distracting and they are horrible without their father or Uncle Chi around. His kid's mothers let his children visit more because they know there's someone to watch them watch while Chi is at practice. It works out well for both of us." Nakita said.

Nakita kissed Chi on the cheek. "Why didn't you ask me to help you with the kids? I was closer and would do anything for any of you, you know that." Matt inquired.

"You and Allyce are too busy Matt. Consuela is raising your children – and she's doing a fantastic job but I want to do it myself, the way mama did with us. Chi does too so we help each other out." Nakita got her dig into Matt.

Matt looked hurt but he didn't say a word. Allyce just sipped on her Coke quietly at the end of the island. As the girls have gotten older, they depended on Consuela more and more. She was there for all the firsts – first step, first word, first tooth, everything. As the girls got older, she coordinated their practices and lessons and made sure that Matt and Allyce knew when performances and games were – although they missed most of them. Nakita was right – Consuela was raising the girls into smart, beautiful, independent young women with a strong sense of respect, responsibility and love of family. She is doing a fantastic job.

I have to say I am impressed with Kita and Chi. They always did work well together but for them to pair up for their children – that was smart. Chi is funny and good with kids but you have to play by the rules. He can be strict – just like Rico. And Kita, Kita is a wonderful mother – kind, caring and nurturing. Their children are truly blessed.

Just as Dira and Matt finished cleaning up the kitchen, "Happy holidays everyone." Travis came through the door.

"Hi baby, how was your flight?"

"It was hours on a plane. What do you think it was like?" Kita shivered as he answered. I never liked the way he talked to her.

"Where are my children?" Travis asked.

"In bed with their cousins."

"Their cousins? Who is all here?" Travis looked around as if he was missing something.

"We all are," Matt said. "All the Lopezes and their children is that a problem for you Travis? You didn't make our sister a Johnson so she should be with her real family."

"You two kill this mess now. I mean it. Travis if you want your children to have their own bed, get a hotel suite. Boys are in one room; girls are in the game room downstairs. Be careful Sampson is down there. Oh, and the next time you think of speaking to my daughter in that manner – think again. You're not in your house, you're in mine and she will be respected here."

"Yes ma'am. You right I'm sorry it's been a long day. Kita baby I'm sorry for snapping at you."

"It's fine Travis." On that note, everyone went to bed. Well, almost everyone.

"Mommy can me and Matt go to the bar for a couple of beers? We won't be gone long." They always knew how to do it. I rarely said no to Malachi.

"Y'all got 'til 3:00 am then I'm sending Sampson for you two."

"Love you Mamasita, see you in the morning. I'll see you in the morning, 3 am I promise and alone."

"Mama can Kita stay at my place tonight? Travis doesn't care." Dira asked.

"I got my grands in the morning anyway. Yeah y'all have a good time. Love you, see you for lunch?"

"Yes, 1:00 pm at the Caruso's downtown." Dira said.

"Yes ma'am." I reminded them. Travis was in the bedroom near the pool. Allyce was down the hall. Finally some sleep. I thought.

It was 4:00 am when I heard a lot of thumping up the stairs. Then I heard deep laughing, then a boom. I got up and ran into the hall. Matthew and Malachi were drunk. Matthew's clumsy butt fell up the stairs and was laying on the landing laughing. It was hilarious.

"Chi get your brother up and get him to his room."

"How mommy? I can barely walk myself." Suddenly their bedroom door opened and out came Allyce.

"Mama could you help me get him up? I'll get him to bed."

"Allyce are you sure you can handle him by yourself?" I asked.

"Yes, ma'am if you can help me get him up off the landing, I'll be fine." So I did and she was right. Once he was upright, Matt could walk with a little guidance from Allyce. You could tell she was used to this kind of behavior from Matt.

I was up again at 8:00 am. It was breakfast with Santa day with the grandchildren. Five girls with mid shoulder or waist length hair to get ready – ooh whew! By 9:45 all the hair was done and the boys were dressed. By 10 we were in the car and on our way. When we arrived at the Windermere Hotel, we were greeted by two Nutcracker soldiers. The girls were in awe. As we headed to the ballroom, ballerinas and sugar fairies gracefully fluttered past. The boys just stood and watched them every time they went by. We had seats near the front. The kids could reach and touch Santa's Workshop. It was a Christmas Fantasy. After a great breakfast of pancakes, sausage, hash browns, coffee for me and juice for the kids it was time. The big man came out and children throughout the ballroom screamed and waved. Santa sat down and pushed the handle to a large golden cage, making the balls inside turn. When it stopped, Santa picked a ball from the cage. Then he said "Attention boys and girls. Each table has a number in the middle of it. If your table number is 5 please step forward."

Monche' said loudly, "that's our table. Come on everybody." I told them to line up from youngest to oldest and that went quicker than I imagined. Monche' was first and they followed in order until it was Isabella's turn.

"What would you like for Christmas Sweetie?"

"For my family to be real." I gasped. Poor Santa had no idea what to say. He gave her a hug; the photographer took an individual photo and a group one of all my grandchildren. I spent a small fortune on copies – 2 of each child and 10 group photos.

Nadira, Nakita and Allyce met us at Caruso's for lunch. Travis had hired a car and driver to bring the children back to my house so we could have a girl's luncheon.   Nadira kept shooting nasty looks at Allyce and Nakita kept looking at her watch.

"Kita do you have an appointment?" I asked.

"No mama. It's just I told Travis I would be home by 3."

"It's only 1:40 Kita, we'll be back by then." I said.

"And what would happen if you were late Kita? Why are you so scared of him? You not the big sister I remember at all." Dira has a very sharp tongue and she had been in rare form ever since they arrived.

"What is your problem Dira? You've been on everybody ever since they arrived. You're not perfect, honey. Don't be bitter just because you chose to be single." I said.

Dira started to cry "Is that what you think? That I chose to be single at this time of year? No mama that's not it, that's not it at all. I left Kendrick because it came out that he had been playin' around on me for about six months. It started when he went to Boston for that job interview. In the end, I caught him in bed with the trick when I went there to surprise him and celebrate his job offer." I felt horrible. Nadira had never said anything about it, not one word. She had suffered this awful betrayal and disrespect all alone.

Finally Kita spoke up. "Dira, contrary to popular belief in this family Travis has never laid a hand on me. He's not like that. He can be mean and when he gets upset, he can say hurtful things. So I try not to upset him that's all." Nakita said sadly.

Allyce chimed in, "does he yell at you or threaten you?"

"He yells sometime. When he gets mad he threatens to take the kids away from me and he could, everything's in his name. I haven't worked in seven years and I haven't finished my degree. On the day we left to come here he told me he won't pay for me to finish my degree. If I want a degree, I need to figure it out. I will, I'll figure out something." Nakita said.

"We'll help you Kita. Matt and I will pay your tuition and books."

"How are you going to speak for Matt? Everything isn't yours Allyce." Nadira asked.

"Nadira, Nakita is his sister too. Normally, I would discuss it with him first but I know he would move Heaven and Earth for either one of you. So yes I'm speaking for him – we WILL pay for it."

"Allyce since you brought it up, how are things with you and Matt?"

"We're a little stressed mama but nothing to worry about. Why do you ask?"

"Isabella made a strange Santa request today and it concerned me a little."

"What did she ask for this time?"

"For her family to be real." Kita spit her water back into her glass. Nadira gave Allyce a dirty look, but said nothing. Allyce began to cry.

"My daughter said that, oh GOD! I never thought she saw." Allyce said.

"That child is wise beyond her years thanks to Consuela. Whatever you two have going on needs to stop now." I said.

"Does anyone need to pick up anything from the shops here or the mall? Kita don't worry I will take care of Travis. You're staying with us today."

"Yes ma'am I would like that."

"Allyce, Dira?" I asked.

"Mama I'm good. I think I'm going home for a little while but I'll be at the house for dinner, it's our turn right – the girls?" Dira asked.

"Okay baby are you sure?"

"Yes ma'am y'all have a good time." Dira kissed Kita and I glaring at Allyce. Dira grabbed her coat and purse and away she went.

"Okay ladies my truck is outside. Kita what's Travis' cell number?"

"Here just use mine mama." She punched him up on speed dial. Travis answered on the first ring.

"Do you know what time it is or are you too stupid to tell time anymore? Where the hell are you? It doesn't matter. If you aren't here in the next ten minutes, the kids and I are going home to pack up and leave."

"Who do you think you're talking to? Act like you're going to take my grandkids anywhere and I will tell Matt and Chi to wear you out. They've been wanting to for years now but I told them no. My daughter is with me. She will stay out as long as she likes and not one word will be said to her about it. Am I clear?"

"Miss Lydia I'm sorry I didn't realize Kita was with you. Of course she should spend time with you that is why we came home. I'll babysit my kids, its fine."

"You can't babysit your own children Travis. Don't speak to my daughter like that again-ever." I hung up before he could respond.

We spent a couple of hours at the mall and got their gifts wrapped there. We decided to pick up Chinese food – the girls were too tired to cook. Dira met us as we were coming in the door. She told the children to get washed up for dinner. We fixed their plates and sent them to the game room with strict instructions not to come back up grown folks were talking. Chi and Matt arrived because they smelled food. Travis came down the stairs after the children were settled in the game room standing in the door way just observing the whole scene. When Miss Lydia saw him she immediately continued from their earlier conversation, "Travis who the hell do you think you are?"

"Mama what's wrong?" Chi asked.

"Mommy what happened? What did he do?" Matt asked too wanting to know what had made his mom so upset.

"Mama you got to see the real Travis today, didn't you?" Dira asked the ultimate question.

"Yes, Dira I did. He talked dirt bad to your sister for no reason and it wasn't the first time according to her. So what do you have to say for yourself?"

"Miss Lydia you need to mind your business and stay out of my family." Travis said in an attempt to control his anger.

"Travis, Nakita, TJ and Tierra are my family so how you treat them will always be my business. If it wasn't for me and her father, she wouldn't exist."

"But TJ and Tierra are MY children. We don't need her. She can come back here with you, I really don't care. I'm not going to marry her. I don't really want her anymore but the kids stay with me." Travis said angrily.

"Whoa Travis, pump your brakes. Did you forget who we are? We made you who you are. My mama's connections got you that lucrative contract with the Patriots as a rookie and those four multi-million dollar endorsements. So if she goes your potential earnings will hit rock bottom I guarantee it. If you have put your hands on Nakita, I promise you will be locked up and your career will be over.

After which Chi and I will beat you unmercifully. That's a promise."

"Why wait? I can whoop him now and when he gets out of jail. I'll take that charge for my sister," Chi chimed in.

"Travis, if my sister wants her children with her, she will have them or I tell everything I saw last fall." Nadira threatened.

"Nadira keep your mouth shut. You remember our deal?"

"You broke that deal when you mistreated her, didn't pay for her schooling or marry her. Deal's over." Dira added.

"Nakita there's a reason why Travis is meaner. He wants someone he can't have. You know how I said I caught Kendrick in bed with a trick? Well he wasn't the only one. I caught a flight to Boston to surprise Kendrick after the second "interview." When I got to the Hilton, I lied to the front desk and told them that I was his wife and I had lost my key card. So they gave me a new one. He was on the 16th floor. On the way up the elevator opened on the 8th floor and guess who got on? Allyce and

Travis!!! They were hugged up in a corner until they realized it was me." Allyce began to cry. Travis shook his head. "I was already trippin' Lopez about that when I got room 1614. I opened the door and found Kendrick in bed with Allyce's assistant Shelby. There. Now there are no more secrets. Make your family real with that one Allyce. Mama I'm sorry." Dira told it all and dropped her own bomb of mass destruction.

"What was the deal Dira? Why did you keep this from the family?"

"Mama he swore it was a one-time thing. That he truly loved Kita and would marry her here for Christmas. He also reminded me of all the years Allyce and Matt had together and asked if I wanted to mess that up over nothing."

Matt looked at his wife, who was still crying at the end of the island. In a restrained angry voice, Matt said "As for you, I'm done. When we get back, the girls and I are leaving. If you don't fight, I will go for joint custody with me as primary. If you fight this and all the other dirty little secrets will come out. Don't bother to threaten me. Most of my secrets are already out and the ones that aren't won't get me fired. Hell some might get me promoted. Consuela tried to warn me but I wouldn't listen. That's why she wouldn't come. She couldn't stand to watch us faking through Christmas. Allyce you can stay until the 27th but after that go find someone to spend New Year's Eve with. Hell you and Travis can spend it together for all I care." Matt yelled.

"EVERYONE SHUT UP!! Y'all makin' plans for me and my life like I'm not standing here. Travis if you want to be gone, please do so. I thought we could work things out, start over make our dream work. If that dream is gone that's all you had to say. As for you, Allyce, I never liked you anyway so it doesn't surprise me that you would pull a stunt like this. Matt, I told you she's an opportunistic trick but you wouldn't listen. Dira you should have never given them Imira. She didn't deserve such perfect little girls. Travis and Allyce deserve each other." Nakita announced.

"Kita what did you say about Imira? What are you talking about?" I asked.

"Mama. Do you remember Armani? The Italian guy Nadira used to date before Kendrick. Well

Allyce and Matt lost their second child – a boy in their fifth month of pregnancy. When Nadira got pregnant she wasn't ready for motherhood, so Matt and Allyce adopted her. Isabella knows but Imira and Illycia don't. She wants to tell Imira but I asked her not to. She feels like all the secrets are tearing her family apart."

"That's why I've been so mad at you Malachi. Armani left when I was five months pregnant. He went back to Italy and I have heard from him once since then. As far as he knows, I was going to raise the baby alone and he could care less. He even refused to sign the adoption papers initially. We had to have it set-up where he gave permission for the adoption under the condition that Imira never be able to find out who he was. And what did you do? Got five babies by five women and not even try to take care of them."

"Speak on what you know on what you know sis. I take care of my children. I speak to all of them every week. Video chat whenever we're on Facebook together. I fly to every performance, game or award ceremony that I can. Those that have step fathers, I work with them and my children's mothers to give them the best life I can. I didn't abandon them. Their mothers and I just didn't work out. That's how I got them here. I had enough frequent flyer miles to get them all to Toledo and then I bought tickets for all of us home. I'm doing the best I can, like mommy and daddy taught us." Chi said.

"Hmmm. Ok does anyone else have anything to say? No. Good. Tomorrow is Christmas Eve can we all act decent for the sake of those children downstairs. No arguing, bickering, or fighting. Travis and Allyce get a hotel room but come back by 2:00 pm tomorrow and not together. The kids don't need to see this mess. Agreed?"

"Yes ma'am."

"Agreed."

"Fine with me."

"I'll stay on my best behavior mama."

"I'll be packed and out of here in 15 minutes." Allyce said moving upstairs quickly with her eyes not leaving the floor.

"I never unpacked but I'll wait for you Allyce." Travis said leaving the kitchen and moving into the living room to wait. And so it was. Everyone had aired their dirty laundry and now we have to survive three to five days with each other.

The next morning was surprisingly normal. Chi fixed all the children Nuevo's rancheros and waffles. Matt took them all ice skating. Nakita and Nadira got all the dessert and candy bar fixings set up and it was gorgeous. It took up the entire dining room table with the leaf pulled out. The children's eyes were huge when they saw it. We made a big cookie tray for Santa and left it on the ottoman next to the tree. After they all fell asleep, we worked together to get all the presents around the tree. We had to move furniture to make it all fit. It was beautiful.

This is my Heaven, my Garden of Eden. You see this is my eternal dream. I died of a heart attack on December 14th as I was wrapping Christmas presents. I now know most of the secrets and I know my children. The four of them together, sooner or later, will let the truth come out before too long. My funeral was on the 21st so as not to upset Christmas for the children. The kids decided to spend Christmas together but of course I wasn't there to referee. Everyone is working through their new roles in the family and they're doing it together, so it all worked out.

This is my Christmas Dream.

Teresa Martin

Christmas

Five days before Christmas and I was curled up on the couch. My head throbbed, my body ached and my cough wouldn't let me rest. *Not the flu!* I thought. *How will I get everything ready for the buffet?*

Our annual Christmas Eve buffet included all the classics: turkey, stuffing, green beans amandine, mashed potatoes, cranberry sauce. My husband, Bob, and our teenage sons, Rob and Derek, prepped the house while I whipped up the feast for our two dozen guests. With my grandmother's lace cloth on the dining room table, I decorated each place setting with my best china and crystal. A vase of fresh flowers completed the scene. It was always so perfect!

'Lord, help me get well…and fast!' I prayed, *'Or our holiday will be ruined.'*

Hours later I was still on the couch, feeling worse than ever.

"We have to cancel the buffet," I told Bob and the boys. "Look at me. I'm flat on my back."

"Don't be silly," Bob said. "We can take care of things."

"Yeah, don't worry, Mom," said Derek.

"We've got this!" Rob added.

I looked up at the three men hovering over me. They had no idea what they were offering to do. "Please just call everyone and cancel. I can't move."

For the next three days, the couch was my home. It was quiet and out of the way. Bob and the boys came and went like usual, except I had the snaking suspicious they were preparing something nice for our less-than-perfect Christmas celebration. Could I even call it that?

By Christmas Eve I finally felt well enough to move around the house a bit. That's when I heard a commotion in the kitchen.

"What's going on in there?" I asked as I got closer. Was that a turkey I smelled cooking?

"One minute, honey!" Bob shouted.

Curious, I went into the dining room, just off the side of the kitchen. The table was set exactly as if I'd done it myself—right down to the vase of fresh flowers. *How sweet*, I thought. But why were there so many place settings?

"C'mon in now!" Bob said.

I walked into the kitchen and there they were: Two dozen of our closest friends, family and neighbors. "Surprise!" they cheered. Bob and the boys had snuck them in through the cellar door. They'd even prepared my usual feast. "We've picked up a thing or two by watching you," Bob said.

Christmas Eve ruined? Not by a long shot. I sure hadn't made it perfect, yet it was. All thanks to the One we celebrate and the family he blessed me with.

Julia A. Royston

A Man for All Seasons

The weather was cool and the trees had no leaves. It was that time again a season with no man. Matthew was the latest to leave and continue the trend. As it goes, after the Labor Day holiday, the calls stop and the dates cease. It happened so often Tamera came up with a slogan, 'it must be fall so he won't call, when it's Spring my phone will ring.' It was depressing but, true. Over the past five years, Tamera dated only half of the year, spring and summer. When she needed a sweater, the man would scatter.

'Not another slogan', Tamera thought to herself as she headed down Main Street in the small town of Orleans, Kentucky. Orleans was a sister city of the big easy but, clearly located in the Bluegrass state.

The smooth jazz version of 'When will I see you again,' filled the car as she pondered, 'Is it too much to ask God for a date that will be around past October 1st?' There was total silence. At thirty-five, Tamera James was relatively attractive, pleasingly plump as her aunts would say, no kids, a librarian at the local public library and the best aunt two nieces and three nephews could ask for. Tamera had one sister and two brothers who were happily married and repopulating the earth. Her mother even remarried after her father passed away ten years ago. Now that was a little disturbing that her mother could marry and she could not.

At times, Tamera felt like she had some type of disease that drove men away. That couldn't be the case, because she attracted them for at least two seasons. There must be a sign posted on her back side that said available for dating only in spring and summer. Men watched her backside enough. If there were something posted on it, they would have noticed and told her about it as they read it out loud.

Somehow it was the same old story. A relatively attractive man walks into the library and approaches the cute librarian at the circulation desk.

Cute Librarian says, 'hello, can I help you find a book today?' Handsome man says, 'yes, I am looking for the latest science fiction books.' About four visits later, while returning library books, the handsome man uttered the awkward statement, 'maybe we can go out some time' or 'can I have your number so we can go out some time? At other times he would say, 'Can you take a look at your schedule and let me know when you are free, so we can go out some time?' 'I will call you.'

'Sure,' said the cute librarian as she received the books and handed him her number. The dating game began. The season must now be spring.

The weather was hot and so was the relationship. They met each other's family, sometimes he begged to stay over and the phone never stopped ringing. Tamera was a good Christian girl but, sometimes the guy was so good that she wanted to cave in but, didn't. She knew that God would forgive her but, could she forgive herself. These thoughts always let Tamera know she was in over her head in heat, not love, and the season changed again, now it was summer. They were adults and kissing was never enough for either of them but, grandmamma taught her that 'she was the marrying kind and she was not the "have fun with and throw away" kind of girl.'

She kept her phone on vibrate during the day and full ring at night. There was nothing, not a call or even a voice mail. She knew the season had changed again. It was October 1st and now it is fall. Tamera always prayed that one day she would have a man in her life not just one or two seasons but, them all.

"What are you and Matthew doing for Thanksgiving?" Katherine, the Technical Services librarian asked, as she uploaded the latest acquisitions onto the library database.

"Who is Matthew?" Tamera's dry tone told details that her words didn't have to utter.

"What happened?" Katherine exclaimed, hushed but, forceful because they were in the library's main room.

"What happens every October 1st? Nothing. No calls, voice mails or dates. Everything stops." Tamera explained.

"Girl, I am so sorry. I thought he was really into you. He seemed like he liked you."

"They all do. He liked me. He said he did. His mama liked me. His daddy liked me. His sister and his brother like me. But, it is always suspicious that when the holidays roll around, nobody likes me. I didn't ask him for one gift. I am not a gold digger. I take care of all of my own stuff. I am not looking for a man to give me stuff but, love. Is that too much to ask?" Tamera waited with a stare that bordered on tears.

"No, it is not too much to ask. Hold on to that thought and don't settle until you get it."

"Well, I will probably be too old to meet him or enjoy it when he comes along."

"No, you will do just fine. I pray hard for you single girls every day."

"Right."

At that moment, a very tall, cocoa brown skinned man walked into the front door. Under her breath Katherine whispered, "Who is that tall, handsome glass of water and how did he get to Orleans. Tamera, girl, this could be your lucky day."

"He looks like something out of the movies. I am not that lucky," Tamera whispered under her breath.

"How can I help you?" Katherine spoke first and asked very sweetly.

"I am looking for the genealogy section," the young man stated.

"I am sorry but, I am not the reference librarian. I am the technical librarian but, I am sure that this young lady right here can help you." Katherine smiled to the gentleman and walked away quickly. Katherine was much taller than Tamera. On the stools at the Reference Desk, she could look directly into the gentleman's face with ease. Tamera needed a step stool for a direct view.

"Yes, sir. Let me get my keys. The genealogy section is in a closed room down the hall. I have to let you in the room. Is there a particular year that you are interested in?"

"I am looking for the birth records from 1978. I have been to the courthouse but, they tell me that you keep them here." Tamera found the keys easily. Darius Mathis stepped away from the desk allowing Tamera to get a whiff of the crisp fresh blue water cologne compared to the stale musty smell of the close genealogy room. Tamera was glad that, in spite of the way she felt, she still came to work looking professional and stylish.

"That is correct. The courthouse is not climate controlled so the records are kept here." Tamera spent time in the men's section of many department stores she thought she smelled 'Dolce and Gabanna Light Blue.' It was not too overwhelming and blended well with his natural body chemistry.

Tamera turned on the light as she walked only a few steps to the birth records. Opening a third drawer, she said, "Here are the records for the 1970's. They are arranged by year for every person that was born in Orleans or the surrounding three counties for any year. If you have any questions, pick up that phone right there and dial 118. The number is also located on top of the phone. If you exit this room the door automatically locks and you can't get back in without me or the key. Well, you could get in with the key but, I need to bring it or someone else could bring it to you. Sorry. I know I sound ridiculous. I will shut up now." Tamera realized how ridiculous she did sound and suddenly got tickled and so did he.

"I am sorry. I didn't mean to laugh at you but, you were laughing so it made me laugh. I got it. What's your name?"

"I'm Tamera. No problem, I get tickled when I am nervous."

"I am Duane Mathis and nice to meet you Tamera. I will need you and the keys for the next

3 days. I am staying here in town to do some research."

"Well, I will leave you to your research and if you need anything, there is the phone."

"Thanks Tamera."

"You are welcome, Mr. Mathis."

"Please call me Duane."

"Okay, Duane." Tamera dipped her head as she left the room with little fanfare and trying not to bump into anything as well. Tamera always seemed to get clumsy when she was nervous.

Chapter 2

Duane Mathis came to the library's Genealogy Room for the next three days. Tamera enjoyed seeing him come through those doors each evening. No major conversation ensued but, general pleasantries were expressed. On the third night, Duane stayed until the library closed.

Walking to the reference desk, he happily announced, "Tamera, I have found what I was looking for and thank you for all of your help."

Tamera surprised herself by being slightly saddened by the news. But, she managed to say, "You are welcome. Have a nice evening." Looking at handsome Duane Mathis for three days had been a wonderful diversion from the usual men in the town who came to the library. Tamera watched as Duane left the library continuing to prepare the library to close. The supplies were restocked and the desk was cleaned off and ready for the early morning shift.

Tamera bent to gather her bag and while hidden from view, heard a voice saying, "Excuse me Tamera." Tamera looked up and then popped up like Jack in the box.

"Oh, hi Duane. I thought you had gone?"

"Well, I had gone but, had an idea. This is my last night in town and I am going to dinner to celebrate my findings. Since you were so helpful, I was wondering if you would have dinner with me tonight to help me celebrate." Tamera was shocked that a man would ask her out, because it was October. This was the wrong season for her to have a date.

"Um, well......." Tamera paused to think for a moment.

Duane hurried the conversation to help her make her decision, "I realize that you don't really know me, but, I promise, dinner will be on me. I just don't want to eat alone tonight and it is my last night in town. Please?"

Tamera looked up into his eyes again and then down at her outfit. She realized that she looked okay for dinner with a stranger. "Okay. Sure, I will have dinner with you tonight to help you celebrate. I have to finish closing the library first."

"Great. Meet me at the Orleans Inn when you are finished. Thank you so much." Duane smiled excitedly and left the library. Tamera stopped straightening the desk and started straightening her mind and wardrobe. A date in October? This was unheard of for Tamera. She had to keep telling herself, 'this is just a dinner between two adults. Don't get too happy. It means nothing. Just like all of the other guys. He'll disappear. He is leaving town the next day.'

Harold the night security officer came by her desk after making a full sweep of the library. "You okay Tamera?"

"Yes Harold, I'm fine."

"You don't look or act fine. You are actually talking to yourself. You'd think you had a hot date or something."

"Something like that,"

"Great. Enjoy!"

"I think I will."

Chapter 3

The Orleans Inn was a combination Mansion/Plantation/Bed and Breakfast.

Breakfast was served for overnight guests. The Inn was open to the public for lunch and dinner.

The bell attached to the front door rang loudly to announce each visitor.

"Welcome to the Orleans Inn." The hostess was Ms. Nosey Nora, as most folks in town called her. Ms. Nora was looking down at the newspaper when Tamera opened the door. The little bell on the door and Ms. Nora looked up from her paper. "Oh hello. Tamera. What brings you to Orleans Inn?"

Realizing that Tamera rarely ate at the Orleans Inn it was a logical question by Ms. Nora. "Hello, Ms. Nora, I am having dinner with one of your guests this evening." Tamera hated that Ms. Nora was on duty, the gossip train was about to leave the station.

"There is nobody here but, that gorgeous Duane Mathis," said Ms. Nora, looking shocked and bewildered. "Ugh, you are meeting him? The Lord must be smiling down on you today."

"Yes, he must." Tamera didn't have time for that woman's attitude today. She walked right past her and into the main room.

"I'm sorry. Right this way." Ms. Nora shuffled her feet to get ahead of Tamera to actually lead the way to Duane's table.

Duane stood as Tamera approached. She tried to remain calm and told herself, 'no expectations. Just enjoy the dinner.'

"Hello and thanks for coming." said Duane who had changed into khaki pants and a blue blazer with sparkling gold buttons compared to the earlier jeans and t-shirt. Tamera exchanged her flats for heels which were in her car trunk. The heels made her two inches taller.

"Thanks for inviting me." Duane pulled out her chair and as Tamera sat down she took in his cologne one more time.

The server came over to their table and their order was taken quickly. Small talk began and Tamera found out some wonderful things about Duane, including why he came to Orleans. He came to find his mother. She let him talk and didn't ask him the name of his mother. Orleans was a very small town. Tamera was quite sure that she would know her. Tonight she wasn't a librarian, researcher or one who answered anybody's questions. Just a girl eating dinner with a nice boy. She could hear the excitement in his voice and see the happiness in his eyes. Even though he had wonderful adoptive parents, he still wanted to meet his birth mother. He stopped talking about his findings and asked Tamera about herself, her interests and how she became a librarian. Duane asked about Tamera's family as well. This was a big switch because most guys were trying to compliment her into some type of sexual action. His real interest in her was refreshing. Duane was a CPA who someday wanted to own his own accounting firm as well as a non-profit consulting firm for small businesses. People need advice prior to starting businesses and he really wanted to help people. Tamera thought his business ideas sounded wonderful. Being a public library librarian was definitely a public service and not about the money. She enjoyed helping people find information that changed their lives as well as support their love of reading. All of the dishes were cleared, only the half-empty water glasses remained because they declined coffee. She finally asked that all important question.

"So when are you going to see her?"

"I don't know yet. I need to go home tomorrow and I'll think and pray about it. I want to call her first and see if she even wants to meet me. I don't know. She might say no."

"Although we've just met, you seem like such a wonderful man. I can't imagine her not wanting to meet you and see how you turned out. At thirteen years old, she couldn't have taken care of you without a lot of help. I am sure that it was the hardest and most important decision she ever had to make."

"Could you have done it?"

"Me with a baby at thirteen? I was a baby at thirteen. Maybe I could, but only with family help. I am still old school. I want a husband and then children."

"I agree. I want a wife and then children." Fortunately, Tamera's chocolate brown skin hid her blushing because Duane looked at her without blinking as he made that statement.

Something changed in the entire atmosphere after that statement. Tamera told herself, 'don't flinch, just breath. Go ahead and ask.' She asked, "So why don't you have a wife and children? What's stopping you?"

"What's stopping me? Me. Even though I had wonderful adoptive parents all of my life, I didn't find out I was adopted until age eighteen. I was applying for a passport and knew where my parents kept their insurance papers, etc. They were out of town and I found my adoption documents. My world crashed in on me. I knew then that I couldn't commit until I was complete or as complete as humanly possible. There were too many questions and too few answers. My parents were sorry, apologetic and so upset about how I found out that I dropped the issue of finding my birth mother until now. It never went away it was just delayed."

"Do you have a girlfriend or special lady in your life?"

"Yes and no."

"What does that mean?" Tamera pressed gently and waited for Duane's answer.

"Yes, this young lady is someone that I go out with occasionally. On the other hand, I have been totally honest with her about my commitment issues. I say no, because I have never fully connected with anyone on any deep level. My heart, body and mind were not 'all in' because I have this unsolved mystery in my life. I feel like I am a puzzle and there is still one piece missing."

Although this were their first time together, Tamera wanted to help Duane sort things out so she pushed again. "And, now?"

"Maybe." Duane's voice trailed off into a low whisper as he looked slightly out the window into the darkness.

Tamera let the word just linger in the air thinking 'Wow, at least he was honest. As honest as he could be.'

"I'm not going to keep you any longer. I am sure that you want to get home and rest from your long day at work." Duane suddenly pulled himself back to the present.

"It was a long day but, I enjoyed your company very much."

"I enjoyed your company as well. I really appreciate you coming out with me tonight on such short notice. You were so helpful and I just wanted to do something to show my appreciation. You ready?"

"Yes." Duane paid for the check as Tamera grabbed her things. He walked Tamera to her car. Once at the car, Duane stretched out his hand for hers and held it as he said, "Good night and have a safe journey home."

"Good night to you too and you have a safe journey home as well. I on the other hand, don't live that far." They both laughed and he watched her drive away until her car was out of sight. Tamera knew it because she watched him standing there through her rearview mirror. When she almost missed a red light, Tamera realized that she must keep her eyes on the road or definitely have an accident. Her night had been so pleasant, it was the only reason she stopping looking in his direction until he was out of sight but never out of her mind.

Chapter 4

The next day Tamera arrived to work a little earlier than usual in a wonderful mood wearing a bright colored blouse and matching skirt. "Look at you lady sunshine. How was dinner last night?" Katherine asked, as she approached the Reference Desk, as she did every morning, putting reference books away that had been cataloged. She was shocked that Katherine would know about last night. "How did you know I went out to dinner last night?"

"Did you forget how small this town is? Nosey Nora is my mom's aunt. Aunt Nora called my mom and then my mom called me. She said, 'it was evident that the two of you enjoyed each other's company.'

"How did she know that?" Tamera turned her head with an annoyed frown to Katherine so fast she almost got whiplash.

"She was watching you the entire night either from the kitchen or the sitting area adjacent to the main room."

"For real. There are no secrets or privacy to be had in this town. It doesn't matter, Nosey Nora will not ruin my day. Ms. Nora needs to go get her a life and not just try to live mine."

"Right. No, there is no privacy unless it is in a book and Nosey Nora is not the hostess at the restaurant, silly. So how was he? Did you have fun? Are you going to see him again? Did you give him your number?"

"Oh my goodness Katherine, you have asked four questions and I haven't even breathed to answer the first one. Question 1, he is wonderful. He is a great guy, gorgeous, spiritual and decent human being. Question 2, he made me laugh, think about some things seriously and reflect all at the same time. Question 3, I probably won't see him again or any time soon, since he doesn't live near here and has a girlfriend. Question 4, he didn't ask for my number, so I didn't offer it."

"Look at you all grown up, acting mature and like a non-desperate single woman. I am proud of you."

"You would be proud. He mentioned a wife and kids and I was excited until I pushed the envelope, as I always do, and found out about a girlfriend. How stupid of me to ruin my fantasy that he was single."

Katherine couldn't help but, laugh at that statement. "Yeah, he might have a girlfriend but, at least, you broke the cycle of someone asking you out in the month of October. That is so great." The two continued talking and laughing most of the morning.

The upcoming weeks were filled with ghosts, goblins, pumpkins and scary stories during story time after school. Tamera wasn't thrilled with Halloween and was glad when all of that ended on November 1st. Duane ran across her mind a few times since that October night at the Orleans Inn. He could have contacted her by calling the library but, Tamera, 'why would he? He has a girlfriend.'

Around November 15, Katherine came by with her highly decorative and creative invitations to her family's Thanksgiving dinner. Katherine was always inviting single, displaced or people with little or no family to join in with her family during the holidays. Tamera thought that was so admirable and people were always appreciative. Tamera had plenty of family. They decided to take a cruise over Thanksgiving break. She loved her family but, seeing everyone coupled up with someone just naturally turned Tamera into the nanny/babysitter. No thanks and not this holiday. So when Katherine passed out her beautifully hand written, calligraphy personalized, invitations with 'special surprise' included, Tamera knew that she had to be there.

"Well, here is your invitation Tamera."

"Thanks, Katherine."

"What are your plans this Thanksgiving?"

"I really don't have any and getting this invitation is going to save me from being home alone with a frozen turkey dinner, hot chocolate and the beginning of the Christmas movies playing on the Hallmark channel."

"I'll have none of that. You will be with me and my family this Thanksgiving."

"What do you want me to bring?"

"Well, don't worry about cooking anything, just bring a couple of bottles of sparkling cider." Katherine said getting more excited about the holidays even though they were still a few weeks away.

"Sounds good to me. I'll come a little early to help out." Tamera was happy that she would be alone.

"Great." Katherine continued talking about the other menu items, decorations, invitations and even activities through the day. Tamera usually stopped by Katherine's house on holidays even when her own family came to visit. Tamera loved the banter, fun, laughter and love she always felt with Katherine's family.

Tamera arrived early as planned to help Katherine in any way possible. She had called her family and they were enjoying 80 degree weather in Mexico. Tamera looked cute in her sweater, matching leggings, gold jewelry and flawless makeup. Tamera carried in two bottles of sparkling cider and a *Kern's Kentucky Derby* pie for dessert, her personal favorite. Katherine's niece opened the door, took her wrap and ushered her to the main room of the day, the kitchen.

"Hey, Tamera. So glad that you could come." Katherine greeted Tamera as she walked in the kitchen. Katherine was dressed in a very festive sweater and leggings with an apron that read 'kiss the cook.' It was evident of all of the hard work that went into preparing for this holiday. The detail in house was decorated to time, money and love. The wonderful smells coming from the kitchen made Tamera's mouth water with anticipation.

"Thanks for inviting me. What can I do to help?" Tamera asked Katherine as she laid her pie and bottles of sparkling wine on the counter.

"Nothing really, just keep me company, unless you want to go watch football."

"No, I am fine right here."

As usual the house was divided by function of room, age groups and activities. Some boys were outside shooting hoops. The girls were upstairs messing with Katherine's daughter's clothes and makeup. The men had the TV and remote in their full control in the family room. The women were controlling the kitchen, as the guests continued to arrive with more food, dessert and other specialties. It was a food lover's paradise. Thanksgiving was about being thankful but, also a day for family, fun, football and yes, the best and most food in one place. Katherine's mother came in the kitchen and said that they were still waiting on one special guest to arrive and then dinner would be served. Katherine eyed Tamera and gave an agreeable, 'yes mother,' from the side of her mouth. Although, the meal was held at Katherine's house, Katherine's mother, Edna, always seemed to be in charge. Katherine gladly let her be in charge.

When the doorbell rang, Katherine's mother, Edna, put both hands at her mouth, burst into tears and whispered, "He's here." I was concerned when I saw Ms. Edna overcome by so much emotion and watched for Katherine's reaction. Katherine gently put one arm around her mother and kissed her on the forehead whispering, "Mom, get the door. He's finally here." Ms. Edna leaped quickly from the kitchen bar stool and said out loud this time, "he's finally here." She was almost gliding down the hallway toward the door.

Katherine announced to everyone, "He's here and let's meet in the living room." All of the family seemed to know exactly what to do except Tamera. She was clueless.

Bewildered, Tamera caught up with Katherine to ask, "Katherine, who's here?" Katherine refused and did not give the secret away to Tamera, even though she was one of her closest friends.

"You'll find out in a minute." Katherine touched Tamera's elbow assuredly as they moved down the short hallway to the living room. The kids were running in from outside, the basement and from the upstairs bedrooms to meet the special guest.

Standing in the back of the living room, Tamera wasn't able to see the guest very well. Since she was shorter than most of Katherine's family, she waited in the corner until the guest came her way. Halfway, into the living room, she looked up and realized that the special guest was Duane Mathis. Ms. Edna hugging him very tightly. All Tamera could think were two things, 'Ms. Edna is Duane's mother? Did you ever think about me?' She was surprised and happy to see him but, slightly miffed that he didn't call her.

Before her question could be answered, there was an announcement from Katherine's mother, Ms. Edna. "I know that some of you have heard my story but, let me tell you the abbreviated version right now. Fifty years ago, I was thirteen years old scared and found out I was pregnant by a fifteen year old boy in my neighborhood. My mother said that since my father was gone she couldn't afford to take care of any more kids so she sent me to my grandmother and they arranged to put my baby up for adoption. The hardest thing I ever had to do was carry that child for nine months but, I never saw or named him." Ms. Edna's voice broke for just a minute and Duane held her hand tighter. One of Katherine's sisters came close for support. There was not a dry eye in the room, including the men. She finally continued. "I am sorry. I get so emotional thinking about it. They put me to sleep and when I woke up, he was gone. I was never to mention it again. I came back to Orleans and it was over. No questions asked. What I didn't know was that she made the adoption closed so I could not find out where my baby was after he was adopted. I was a minor and she controlled everything. Since I had no name and did not know whether it was a boy or girl, I couldn't find him. About a month ago, my baby found me. I had always wondered what happened to my baby. Now, I know. He is a handsome young man." Her tears began again. "I am most thankful that he agreed to come spend Thanksgiving with us. Duane would you like to say something?"

"Yes, just that I thank you all for welcoming me with open arms. I look forward to many more holidays together. I appreciate it." Ms. Edna broke down again with tears of joy. She was truly humbled and grateful. Katherine had another brother. The entire family welcomed Duane with hugs, tears and introductions. Tamera cried as well. She cried for Katherine, her mom and seeing a family reunited. It was wonderful. What a Thanksgiving!

Duane finally made his way to Tamera. "Hi, how are you?"

"I am fine. How are you?"

"Great now. I met my mom, my other siblings and I am so glad to see you."

"It is good to see you again as well. All I can say is wow and congratulations. "

"Thank you. I prayed about seeing my birth mother and here is the result."

"Fantastic! I had no idea that I would see you on Thanksgiving."

"I know you didn't but, I did."

"How?"

"A little birdie told me."

Duane tilted his head slightly and motioned only with his eyes toward Katherine, who was walking past them.

"Oh, a little birdie told you, huh?"

"Yes." Katherine walked by with her head down smiling not making eye contact.

"Katherine, you knew and didn't tell me?"

"Well, no, I couldn't because I promised my mother. I love you Tamera but, I love my mother more and I promised. Are you surprised?"

"Triple surprised. I totally understand but, I will get even." They both laughed and with a quick hug, Katherine winked while walking away. Duane and Tamera sat down on the bench seat at the window while he continued telling his story. The sun was going down behind the big oak tree reflecting its dimming light into the pond.

"I want you to know that I thought about you a lot over the past few weeks. I intended to call but, realized that I needed to take care of some things first before contacting you. As soon as I got back home though, a lot of things happened. The young woman I had been seeing broke up with me. She told me that she had reunited with an old boyfriend after attending a reunion. That relationship is officially over."

"Oh, I am sorry to hear that."

"I'm not. She deserved a whole man committed to her and that wasn't me."

"How long did you date her?"

"One year."

"Wow, that's something. I can't seem to date someone more than two seasons of the year."

"What?"

"Never mind, that's a long story for another time. What else happened?"

"The next day, my firm sent me on special assignment to China for 3 weeks."

"Congratulations that must have been great."

"It was great but, I left the same day that I arrived to work with no pre-planning I just packed up and left. When I returned, I was promoted to partner to open a branch of the firm in Branford, Kentucky."

"Our Branford, Kentucky?"

Duane held Tamera's gaze and said, "Now, it truly is our Branford, Kentucky. I packed up my condo and moved to Branford last week."

"Really?" Tamera couldn't believe she said out load exactly what was going on in her head.

"Really. My adoptive parents aren't very happy that I won't be close to them but, happy that I won't be alone. I will be close to my other mom, my extended family and hopefully to you." Tamera felt a hot blush come on her face and she was thankful again for the chocolate skin. Could this be her man for all seasons? She didn't know but, remained hopeful. Ms. Edna called out that dinner was ready to be served and eaten. Charles, Jr., who was the next oldest, led us in the blessing of the food.

Duane stood, reached out his hand to help Tamera off of the bench and asked, "Are you ready for this?"

"Yes, I am." Hand in hand, the two made their way to Katherine's very crowded dining room.

Julia A. Royston

A Man in the Off Season

You asked boldly for the numbers

That make my phone ring

It might have been March or maybe May

I don't care, I know it was spring

You called faithfully

At least twice a day

You called to hear my voice

Even with chocolate skin, I blushed anyway

The fourth of July

The fireworks flew

This was going pretty good

The family inquired and wholeheartedly approved

Then came August

Back to school, pencils and crayons

I was busy, preparing

But, still kept my ringer on

The calls were fewer and far between

I didn't notice at first

We met on the weekends

No arguments or no words said were mean

But, October came around

Now, I needed a sweater

To hear your voice I called you first

When did you become a texter?

I should have known then

It was the beginning of the end

The big and important holidays

Were about to begin

Big family gatherings

Fall Festivals and Thanksgiving

The biggest gift day of them all

Christmas and Santa making several trips to the mall

For a solid six months, nothing at all

No text, no tweet and certainly not a call

From October to March, no smoke signal or sign

No calls or dates, it's over, the deadline

How do you do that?

What does it take?

To forget somebody

Their number to forsake

Don't you miss my voice?

The laughter and witty conversation

I know it's by choice

But, I deserve some explanation

Your phone is on

I called it twice

Stop being a jerk

I'm trying to be nice

Just say let's end it

Just say we're through

Don't ignore my calls

I'm not stalking you

You asked for my number

You called me first

You told me I was thunder

And the quench of your thirst

Nobody made you

Or, stuck a gun to your head

To take me out was your choice

It came out the mouth at the front of your head

Now winters through

Snow is gone

The birds are chirping

Trees now have leaves to dawn

I hear the ring,

My phone is loud

The number is old

The gall, the nerve He's calling me now

You're kidding me right

You think I might

Want to believe you

And pick up the receiver

I'm scrolling and deleting

Your number and handle for tweeting

You're unfriended and blocked

All Social Media and Inbox

You forgot me then

I forget you now

My new man is Ben

So let the games begin

Made in the USA
Columbia, SC
20 September 2023

23038743R00078